DATE DUE

ARCHIE, FOLLOW ME

LYNNE CHERRY

Dutton Children's Books   New York

To Dr. Sidney Diamond, whose love for his family
and friends, for his patients, for knowledge, and
for life was a joy and an inspiration.

Copyright © 1990 by Lynne Cherry
All rights reserved.

Library of Congress Cataloging-in-Publication Data
Cherry, Lynne.
Archie, follow me/ by Lynne Cherry.
p. cm.
Summary: A little girl describes her relationship
with her cat.
ISBN 0-525-44647-8
[1. Cats—Fiction.]   I. Title.
PZ7.C4199Ar   1990
[E]—dc20   89-77160   CIP   AC

Published in the United States by
Dutton Children's Books,
a division of Penguin Books USA Inc.
Designer: Susan Phillips
Printed in Hong Kong by South China Printing Co.
First Edition   10 9 8 7 6 5 4 3 2 1

Every day when I wake up, my cat Archie wakes up too.

Wherever I go he follows me—as I have my breakfast,

brush my teeth, and as Mom braids my hair.

He watches me run
for the school bus.
Where does she go
all day, he must wonder.

When I come home, there is Archie, waiting.

He runs to me, jumps into my arms, and purrs.
I think he's glad I'm home.

"Come follow me!"
I say. So down
to the woods we go,
past Mr. Young's
snapdragon patch,
along the creek
where the wildflowers
bloom.

All the animals are hiding.

But I know they are watching us.

Archie sits so still
that the animals forget
he is there.
Slowly they come out
of their hiding places.
I sit as still
as a statue, too.
Then birds begin to sing.
We sit.
The squirrels chase each other.
We sit.

A pheasant with her chicks glances our way.
She stops and cocks her head.

I hold my breath. Archie doesn't move.
She comes closer—close enough to touch me!

I catch Archie
in mid-leap!
The pheasant
and her chicks run
squawking and cheeping
into the underbrush.

"Follow *me!*" I say to Archie.
We cross the creek by the weeping willows

and creep into our hideaway for a rest...

until Mom's dinner bell
calls us home.

Every night when it gets dark,
Archie jumps up to the window.

Where does he go? I wonder.
He turns and looks at me as if to say, "Follow *me!*"

So I do.
Through the yard,
down the hill,
I follow him
in the moonlight.
He disappears
under the bushes
covered by
morning glory vines
and goes down a hole.
So down the muddy hole
I slide, too.

At the bottom, we meet one, two, three—more than a dozen pairs of cat eyes. I see Archie's friends Dusty, Tuffy, Skunkie, Pumpkin, and Mystery!

But I know I should be sleeping,
so I say, "See you in the morning."

Walking back,
I think of the ways
Archie and I
find out about
each other's world.
I've seen the night
through a cat's eyes,
heard the sounds
of the forest
with a cat's ears,
and smelled
with a cat's nose.

So I'll watch Archie and he'll watch me,
and I'll follow Archie and he'll follow me.
And who knows where we will lead each other
and what we will discover tomorrow.